P9-CQG-146

THE SORCERER'S APPRENTICES
NIGHT
LIGHTS

THE SORCERER'S APPRENTICES

ILLUSTRATED BY

MARTIN SPRINGETT

NICHOLAS STUART GRAY

St. Martin's Press/New York

Published by St. Martin's Press
175 Fifth Avenue, New York, New York 10010.

The NIGHT LIGHTS series is produced by Armadillo Press.

Library of Congress Cataloging-in-Publication Data

Gray, Nicholas Stuart.
The sorcerer's apprentices.

(Night lights series)
Summary: Eager to learn magic, two young boys pit their wits against those of a more powerful wizard.
[1. Magic—fiction. 2. Wizards—fiction]
I. Title.
PZ7.G78So 1986 [Fic] 86-31581
ISBN 0-312-57282-4

Book design and original NIGHT LIGHTS concept by:
Dave Orlon

Production: Richard Salvucci

Typesetting: Robert K. Wiener/ARCHITYPE
Special thanks to Carol and Steven, Parkinson International.

Manufactured in South Korea

THE SORCERER'S APPRENTICES
NIGHT LIGHTS

Once, and not so long ago, there was a sorcerer called Alain. The turrets of his castle towered high amongst high mountain peaks. Enchanted peaks, at that, set there by Alain to guard his gates; and in a century so distant that even he had almost forgotten they were not real.

Having become the recognized authority on magic in the country to which he had brought his castle in the mountains, he was a busy wizard. As his fame still grew, people came from everywhere to consult him. And being overworked, he became irritable. Sometimes his magic took a malicious turn. He began to get a bad name.

One evening he was snatching at an uncustomary moment of peace. He sat in the entrance hall of his castle, which was library, livingroom, and reception chamber, and he was reading a book. Suddenly his head went up; he listened intently for a moment and then spoke to the deerhound at his feet.

"Go and open the door!" he snapped. "The boy is nearing the last of the hundred steps."

The hound went loping away. Alain rapped a short spell at the fire, and it roared up the chimney in an agitated burst of activity.

Then there came the sound of plodding footsteps. A boy came into the hall, and looked all round him with expectant, eager brown eyes. He seemed about fifteen, and his hair was brown, too, and very untidy. His nose was short and broad. He was not at all good-looking, but somehow likable. When he saw the sorcerer he gave a gasp, and visibly his weariness fell from him. He darted forward—and stopped—and bowed.

He received no encouragement from the sorcerer. Alain did not even glance up from his book. But the boy was not put off. He came a little closer, and bowed again. He said breathlessly, "Please—I want to be a sorcerer. May I learn from you? Please—I've come such a long way to find you."

Getting no sort of answer, he fell silent. He stood and stared at Alain. But the eyes of the sorcerer never shifted from the golden letters of his book, though he did shift one shoulder, rather crossly, so that his white fur tunic rippled in the firelight, and faint tracings gleamed on his belt as if they were gold thread, or magic. In fact, they were both.

The boy stretched out his hand timidly toward the fire. Steam was rising from his clothes. He had come through rain and snow; he was hungry; he was tired; he was beginning to feel anxious.

At last the sorcerer spoke. "I have wondered what to do about you," said he, "since you set your feet on my mountains."

"Oh—you knew I was coming here?"

"I am not a novice!"

"No, indeed not! You're very, very clever," said the lad soothingly. "And you're extremely efficient, and—clever . . ."

Alain stared at him, and his voice tailed off. After a moment he gulped and said timidly, "My name is Martin. Please don't send me away."

The sorcerer looked cautious. "What about your parents? Is it their wish that you should take up magic? It's a dog's life," he ended dourly.

"I only have an uncle, sir. He doesn't care anything about me, as long as I give him no trouble. I've just run away. He won't mind."

"I see."

"My uncle has a farm. I worked there since I was—since my parents—I worked very hard, sir. I could—I could milk cows for you," said Martin hopefully.

The wizard cut him short. "I obtain milk by more complex methods," he snapped. He stared at the fire, frowning. Then he said, rather moodily, "Very well. Stay and learn—if you've got the wit. And," he added in a stern voice, "see that you give *me* no trouble, either."

"Oh, I will! I mean, I won't! I mean, I'll try. Thank you, sir—oh, thank you!"

The sorcerer found himself with an assistant, and even more work on his hands.

Martin loved magic. He worked hard at it. But his enthusiasm outran his discretion. He had to be watched constantly. No amount of warning prevented him from rash experimenting, and he was frequently in trouble. Even an evening spent as a footstool under the feet of Alain did little to dampen his eagerness for sorcery.

One day he was crouching before the fire, saying spells to it. The flames had turned a painful magenta and were going upward in spirals. Excited by this, Martin racked his brain for further charms. The sorcerer had gone out, so he felt free from supervision. He felt daring. Jumbled runes and spells poured from his lips. And suddenly a dreadful face appeared in the flames, and mouthed back at him silently.

"Good gracious!" said Martin, recoiling. Then he rallied. "Speak to me, Face," said he.

It didn't. So he used the spell that was to make eggs confess how long they had been laid.

"Higgle-huggle-hoo-hoo-hig."

He said it again and again. Then he got slightly muddled, and said, "Huggle-hoggle-hig-hig-hook!"

"Eh?" said the Face.

"What?" said Martin.

"Don't be ridiculous. *You* must question *me*," snapped the Face. "Only one question, that's the rule. *And* you can't ever use that huggle-hoggle rubbish on me again."

"I didn't mean to, anyway. I didn't know it would do anything—"

"Well, it did, didn't it! Oh, come on! Hurry up, I haven't all day to waste, gossiping with silly little boys!"

"Don't rush me."

Martin pushed his hair out of his eyes with one hand, gazing excitedly at the Face. With one ear he was listening all the time for the soft tread of the sorcerer. He meant to get the fire straightened out before Alain saw it. He had not minded being a footstool much, but preferred being himself. He said, "I wonder where he is? I don't want him coming back before I think of a good question."

"You've asked it," said the Face, pulling some extraordinary grimaces. "And I'll answer. He's in the hidden tower, talking to his prisoner."

"Hey! That was only a thought, not a question!"

"It counted as a question."

"You cheated. I meant to ask about the Stone of Alchemy."

"Too late! Yah!" screamed the Face in a frenzy of glee. "You asked, and I answered, and much good may it do you! Yah! Boo! Sucks!"

It bobbed up and down, and vanished.

Martin muttered some tag-ends of other spells. The fire turned black, and half a dozen eggs shot from it, tittering. They burst on the hearth, and the fragments collected themselves, grew feathers, and shot up the chimney.

Then Alain came. He sat down and opened a book. Martin murmured and whispered to the fire until it settled into a fairly normal condition. Just occasionally an odd-colored puff of smoke burst from it. When this happened, Martin glanced sideways at his master. But the sorcerer affected not to notice the smoke or the glance.

After a while he gave Martin a short dissertation on the theory and practice of magic, with some simple examples. The boy listened, open-eyed and mouthed, forgetting to take notes or remember what he was told. Somewhere at the back of his mind he was wondering about the hidden tower—about the sorcerer's prisoner.

"... and on this word, it will come to you," said Alain.

And he spoke the word, in his deep, soft voice.

In the fire, where the Face had been, a great bird began to take shape. It was made of brass, or gold, and as it grew it sang. Then it spread its wide clanging wings, and the Phoenix glided to the arm of the sorcerer's chair.

Breathless with admiration, Martin stretched out a hand. He got a hard smack from Alain.

"Fool, it's red-hot!" snapped the wizard.

Yet he stroked the fabulous bird himself, and it shot glitters of flame from its hooded eyes.

Martin, snubbed and cross, muttered his little egg-spell.

The Phoenix clicked its beak and squawked, "A hundred years ago."

The sorcerer made two movements with his left hand. With the first, the Phoenix disappeared. With the second, Martin turned into a small, furry rug.

Alain put both feet on the rug, dropped his chin on his hand, and settled to a quiet evening with his book.

Some days later the sorcerer informed his apprentice that he had an engagement with the king of a local country. He strongly advised Martin to behave himself during the time he would be left alone in the castle. Martin promised to try. Alain departed. Martin began at once to search for the hidden tower.

After a few hours, the boy realized it was more difficult than he'd hoped. The tower was not merely hidden. It was invisible. Undaunted by the obvious drawbacks, he started searching for a secret entrance.

Many times he had been warned against the dangers and mysteries that

lurked in that rambling castle. Unknown powers that would tolerate no meddling by a novice. Martin decided to forget the warnings. In this he succeeded instantly.

He wandered through labyrinthine corridors. He opened unlocked doors, and doors with locks—sometimes with one of the keys he had taken from the wizard's study, and sometimes with spells that he happened to remember. He found many strange things, and many horrible things, and many surprising things. But, late in the afternoon, he was no nearer to finding the hidden tower.

Just occasionally it crossed the lad's mind that he was tampering with trouble. If anything dreadful happened, the sorcerer would not know, and could not help. Martin shrugged his shoulders.

"One must take chances, if one wishes to learn," said he.

As twilight fell he came into the long hall that led to the sorcerer's private rooms. No one but Alain ever entered there. Even the rash Martin quailed a little at what he meant to do.

The door across the passage was fastened with nine locks. They would only open for nine separate spells, none of which were known to Martin. He felt all round the edges, but there seemed to be no crack between the bronze door and the iron lintels. Martin stamped his foot. He lay down flat and tried to peer underneath, but all he found was a piercing draft that made his eye water.

"Fiddle!" he said crossly.

Then he heard the faintest of all possible footfalls. He sprang into an alcove that was near the door. Holding his breath, he saw the wizard's great, white hound, Dalgard, come slowly along the corridor and stop in front of the door. There was a long silence. The tongues of the nine locks clicked, one by one. The door swung open. The hound paced forward into the dark, and the boy slipped in behind him. The door thudded shut.

There were nine clicks from the locks.

Martin stood blinking at the two distant flecks of light that began to glow through the darkness. He was remembering suddenly all the warnings he had been given—remembering the forbidden place where he now stood—and his enthusiasm for finding the hidden tower waned slightly.

A greenish sort of glow flickered over everything. The flecks of light brightened. Some way off, Martin saw a stone couch, and a gigantic black cat that stretched full-length upon it. The two lights were the blazing lights of its green eyes. The whole great hall was lit by them now. Many of the things that Martin saw he could not even name. Odd shapes wavered and formed and faded. Batlike wings moved across the vaulted roof. Shadows of thin great hands stretched from behind pillars and tapestries and curiously shaped furniture. Various rugs twitched a little on the stone-flagged floor. There were steps leading up to the couch, and on one of the lower treads crouched a sphinx made of green marble. Its smile was mocking. Martin thought it was a statue, until it narrowed its eyes.

Out of the rustling and echoes and whispers of the eerie place, the cat spoke.

"Well, boy?"

And Martin, being too startled to think of any excuse, told it the truth. "Please—I'm looking for the hidden tower."

"Why?"

"Er—" but again the boy could think of no convincing reason but the true one, "—well—to see the sorcerer's prisoner."

"Why?"

But Martin had never thought as far ahead as that. He rubbed his brow nervously. "It—seemed an interesting thing to do."

"Your master would not be pleased."

"Oh, wouldn't he?" said Martin with great innocence.

"I am almost certain he would not."

The great cat stretched out a paw and let the claws show for an instant.

"Er—suppose he doesn't find out?" said Martin, and added daringly, "Suppose you tell me where the tower is, and I just go and have a quick look, and come away, and never say a word about it? How would that be?"

He gave a small gasp at his own daring. The cat seemed slightly taken aback too. Silence fell again, except for the rustlings and small whisperings in the shadows. The boy glanced uneasily across his shoulder. Over in a corner some lengthy creature dragged itself into deeper darkness, away from the light of the cat's eyes, and it left behind a trail of glittering slime.

The cat spoke at last. "Very well, boy. You shall find the tower."

"Oh, how kind—"

The cat hissed at him. "You poor little fool," it snapped, "you are risking madness and death! You shall take the consequences of your own rashness. Find the tower. Find the prisoner. But—you must not speak one word to him. Not one word. If you do, you'll bring all the dreadful black enchantment of the castle round your ears. The smallest spell in this hall could destroy you. The twitching of one hair of my tail could reduce you to a handful of gray powder! But—you belong to the sorcerer. You may live, this once. If you take my advice, you'll think no more of the hidden tower. You'll go back unharmed to the places that you know."

"But you promised—you said I could find the—"

"I know I did!" snarled the cat. "I have also offered you some good advice. However, if you persist, have it your own silly way. Go to the tower. But, for your life, remember—not one word to the prisoner there. Follow Dalgard."

Martin found the hound was standing beside him. He put a hand on the thick fur of his neck, and went with him across the room toward a blank

stone wall. The darkness gathered round him as he went farther from the eyes of the cat. Things drew away as he approached them, but they did him no harm. Once something hissed at his feet. The hound growled, and the hissing died away in a long moan.

When he came to the wall, the hound nosed it, and suddenly there was a black arched opening. Martin gasped. Dalgard slipped from under his hand, and the boy found himself climbing a winding stairway, alone and in pitch darkness.

After a time, he came to the slit of a window, and he saw the sky. Deep, indigo blue above, lightening to green in the west, and a star on the horizon.

Then he stopped before a door of solid iron. There was a chain welded to the center of it, and a great lock on the chain. But, to the boy's surprise, the chain had not been put through the staple on the lintel. It hung loose. The door was not, in fact, fastened. It could be pushed open. Martin pushed it.

The room in the tower was circular. There were thin windows round about, and a fireplace in the rough stone walls. Logs burned there. And torches glowed in cressets. All the flames, from the fire and torches, were sending up a thin, green, sweet-smelling smoke. Martin crossed the floor, glancing interestedly at carved chairs and a table laden with glass goblets, plates, and bowls of fruit. And he stood by a narrow bed and looked at the sorcerer's prisoner.

He lay on his back, an arm across his face. There was golden embroidery on his black doublet, and a ruby ring on his hand.

Martin opened his mouth to ask if the prisoner slept. Then he shut it quickly. Somewhere in the back of his brain a voice told him that—for some reason forgotten—it would be best not to speak.

The prisoner sat up abruptly, and stared. He was a young man with hair the color of red dust, and seal-gray eyes. He looked extremely surprised.

"Who are you?" he demanded.

Martin shook his head and pointed at his own tight-shut mouth. This seemed to irritate the other. He frowned.

"Don't stand making faces at me!" he snapped. "Answer me; who are you? Are you under a spell? Or raving mad?"

Martin made soothing gestures at him. His efforts made no improvement on the prisonser's temper. He pointed at his mouth again and smiled placatingly. The young man jumped to his feet, and boxed his ears.

"Don't!" said Martin indignantly. Then he clapped both hands across his mouth. He gazed at the prisoner with round and horrified eyes. "I talked," he mumbled indistinctly.

"About time," said the other. "Now will you stop being aggravating, and answer some questions!"

"I was told—I mustn't speak to you. Something will happen! Something dreadful."

"Another slap from me," said the young man angrily.

"Well—it's done, now," said Martin. "I suppose I can't make it worse by talking, now—"

"Who are you? Who sent you here?"

"I'm Martin. I'm an apprentice of the great sorcerer, Alain."

The boy was speaking half below his breath, afraid—now that it was too late—of what he had done. The prisoner looked at him with some scorn.

"Do you fear Alain?" said he. And he sat down on his bed again and hooked one knee across the other with the greatest nonchalance. "Although he keeps me prisoned here," he said, "he doesn't cause me the slightest qualm, sorcery or no sorcery. What is more—" and he lifted his voice—"I would tell him so to his face." He glanced toward the door, as if he expected someone to be standing there.

"He's not with me," said Martin thankfully. "And he didn't send me. I came on my own—just from—well, curiosity. And now I think I'd better be going, sir, if you'll excuse me—"

"Well, I won't!" said the other, sounding cross. "I'm sick of being here alone, with no one to talk to. I've been alone here for years!"

"That's not true," said Martin, shocked. "The sorcerer was here the other day. A face told me."

"You're deranged!" said the prisoner. He turned his head away and began to pick at a tassel on his pillow. He suddenly seemed lonely and unhappy. Martin went a little closer.

"Why are you here, sir?" he said.

Without looking round, the young man spoke sullenly: "I am Avenel, the son of the king."

Martin's jaw dropped. Then he remembered his manners, and bowed.

"Your Highness," said he.

"Don't be such a fool," snapped the other. "I'm nothing now but a prisoner!"

"Er—how did it come to happen?"

Martin was nearly bursting with curiosity. But the prince sprang to his feet, and went to one of the windows, and stood twisting a button on his sleeve. His head was bent so that his face could hardly be seen in the shadow of his red and torch-lit hair.

"Please—" said Martin. "I would like to know, sir—"

"It's none of your business."

"Of course not. But I would like—"

"Oh—! Well, it went like this," said the prince. "I'm interested in magic—"

"Like me."

"What? Oh, very likely. And one day—" The young man lifted his head. But he did not look at Martin. He scowled at the night sky, and the stars. "I had heard tales of the sorcerer, Alain. And I came here to his castle, and

demanded that he teach me his power."

"How bold. I *begged* it. And did he?" said the boy.

The prince gave a small cough. "In a way," said he. He hit his fist on the embrasure of the window, and then wrung his hand and rubbed it with the other. He said: "He laughed at me. He called me names. 'Insolent—overbearing'—he was extremely rude to me! He sent a message to my father—by a bat, believe it or not—saying he quite agreed, and to keep me here until I learned manners. What about that, then?"

"How long—"

"Three months, now."

"Then it looks as though you haven't learned better manners."

Martin ducked as the prince snatched up a cushion from a chair and hurled it at his head.

"You did ask!" he squeeked.

"Go and tell your master," said Avenel through his teeth, "that I will not be dictated to, or bullied by any evil old sorcerer! He can keep me here forever before I'll apologize to him! Be off with you, boy, and tell him what I say."

"No, no—" cried the apprentice in alarm. "I don't want him to know I've seen you. He'll be so cross. And—oh, good gracious!—I wasn't to speak at all, and I've been—"

"Who said you weren't to speak, if *he* doesn't know you came here?"

"An enormous great black cat."

Martin told the prince about his search for the hidden tower, and how he had come to find it. And Avenel suddenly gave an exclamation, and ran across to the door.

"Then it isn't locked!" he cried dramatically. And he flung the door wide open.

"Here!" said Martin weakly.

The other gave him a flashing grin across one shoulder.

"You'll cop it!" said he. And away he went, down the winding stairway.

"Good gracious!" sighed Martin. He went after the prince, with a sinking heart.

When they came to the archway leading into the hall of the sorcerer, the prince stopped abruptly, and Martin walked into him and clutched his sleeve for support.

"Is—is the cat looking at us?" whispered the boy.

"Yes," said Avenel briefly.

He went on, and Martin followed without enthusiasm.

The great hall was now full of light. Green and gold, flickering in the vaulting of the high roof like the reflections from moving water. The black cat lay on the couch. The smile of the sphinx was even more mocking. Things slid away into corners, leaving strange shadows showing on the walls.

The prince stared all round, with bright eyes. Then he crossed the floor to a table, whose legs were carved like the feet of lions. And he stood looking at a book that lay there; a book with golden clasps on its cover; a book with glittering words on its cover; a book with glittering words on its spine; a book that was closed.

"Leave it alone, do!" said Martin. "Oh, please, sir, don't go touching things. Do go back to your prison, like a dear good prince. I'll get into such trouble if you go on so!"

It had come to him, rather belatedly, that sorcery is not a thing that can be mastered by force.

"What rubbish you talk," said the prince. "How can the silly old sorcerer really harm us? He only knows a few small spells, and runes and such. This"—and he waved a lordly hand at the terrible great hall—"this is

all hocus-pocus! Tricks to frighten the ignorant. Pooh!" said he, and opened the book.

There was a tremendous flash, and the green sphinx leaped onto the table in a bound and stared at them.

"What do you ask?" it cried in a voice of avalanche.

No one answered.

Martin glanced at the prince. But that gentleman seemed a little less sure of himself at the moment. "Go away," he said weakly.

The sphinx lifted a scornful lip and vanished.

After a slight pause, Avenel pulled himself together and gave a shaky laugh.

"Not bad—for a trick," he said.

He turned another page of the book.

The room grew darker. There was a faint smell of singeing. Something laughed quietly. Avenel gave a look around, and Martin clutched at the sleeve of his tunic.

"Please—oh, please stop," he whispered.

There was a whirring noise overhead, and the prince slammed the book shut. Then he sniffed and looked at the boy.

"Now listen," said he. "If there is truth in magic, we want to find out all we can. And this is a fine opportunity. You are poor-spirited, Martin," he said in a withering tone.

He then took a deep breath and opened the book again.

The whirring noise recommenced, and a voice from somewhere in the shadows of the vaulted roof said, "Yes?"

They looked up, but saw nothing that might speak. Only shifting shadows. They looked at one another, and each made a slight grimace of alarm. Then Avenel bent his handsome head and read aloud the words of the page under his hand. All around rose a faint howling that added itself to his voice like a horrible echo. And a gray cloud filtered up through the stone floor, and floated over them, and rained on them silently and wetly.

Avenel turned up his collar with one hand and went on reading. Even the admiring Martin realized this was sheer bravado. The howling grew louder until the prince was shouting the final words on the page. The room began to spin. The whole room—faster and faster.

From amid the howling, the pouring sound of the rain, the clatter of falling books and instruments, came the voice above their reeling heads that said monotonously, "Yes? Yes? Yes? Yes?—"

Avenel was clutching the table for support, his eyes tightly shut. And Martin was rolling about on the floor at his feet, clutching at his ankles to steady himself while debris tumbled all about; then an iron-clasped book fell from a shelf, bounded over the floor, and hit him a great thump on the side of the head.

"Fiddle!" shrieked Martin. "Fiddle, and fiddle, and fiddle!"

The room stopped spinning and burst into flames.

"Oh, very clever!" said Avenel in a gasp.

"Yes? Yes? Yes? Yes?—" droned the voice from the roof.

"You shut up!" snapped the prince.

Something laughed again in the flame and shadow. A quiet laugh, amused and sardonic.

The rain falling into the leaping flames made a great hissing and splutter. The prince threw back his head as a spurt of fire leaped to flick at his cheek.

"Look in the book again!" yelped Martin, who had burnt his hand on a glowing bit of rug. "Find another spell, can't you, if you're so much cleverer and bolder than I!"

The prince flung open the book rather defiantly and at random. He looked distastefully at the words that were written in letters of fire. But he read them in a hurried gabble. And Martin burnt himself again and shouted

his egg-spell at the top of his voice.

A gale came shrieking through the hall, with thunder pealing, and lashed up the rain to a torrent. Half-invisible monsters were twisting and vanishing and reappearing in the sudden flashes of lightning that tore through the storm.

Avenel said something in a very small voice.

Martin added a color-spell in a whisper.

The lightening turned magenta, and the room turned sideways.

Now the floor sloped steeply toward the arched windows. Through these, as they whirled round and round, the sorcerer's apprentice and the prince caught glimpses of the mountain peaks—which were growing smaller and smaller—more and more distant . . .

"The castle is flying away with us!" moaned Martin.

A star crashed through the roof and burst in a cloud of choking smoke. From this came a thing that hovered for a moment, and cackled, and faded out.

Martin clutched the prince's boots and the legs of the table. But all of them were starting to slide down over the floor toward the windows.

"Avenel—!" wailed the boy. "If we fall through we shall fall through miles of air, onto the peaks of the mountains!"

"I realize that," said the prince.

Something laughed again.

The slowly sliding table caught against an uneven stone and fell on its side. Martin wedged himself among its legs and felt the claws of the wooden lions close on him. The prince had stumbled to his knees. And they slid on.

"My lord Alain—" wept Martin, "help! Please come back and help!"

Through the deafening and blinding chaos that surrounded them, he heard the prince say in a breathless voice, "Spare us—let us off—this once."

Two steady, green lamps began to shine through the tempest. Among the flames, the rain, the falling debris, the dreadful slant and spin of the hall, the black cat lay calm and unconcerned on its couch. Its eyes were the lamps. It stretched out a paw, opened its mouth to yawn, and spoke one word of enchantment.

The room lurched, and righted. The wind rushed and shrieked, and was still. Everything went quite silent.

The cat laughed, a quiet laugh, amused and sardonic.

And it changed its shape and became the sorcerer.

Martin stumbled to the couch, and feel in a heap beside it. He had never been so glad to see anyone in all his life.

"I enjoyed your magic," said Alain.

"I didn't," said the boy. "And it was none of mine, sir. You did it all from the start."

The sorcerer smiled. He turned his brilliant eyes on the prisoner. The prince drew a long breath, got to his feet, and straightened his shoulders. He looked back at the wizard, rather crossly.

"All right," he said. "I asked for it. But I tired of being prisoned."

"The door was never locked," said Alain quietly. "You could have walked out whenever you chose. You knew that."

The prince gave a lopsided smile. "Yes," he said, "I knew. But how tame a finish." He bowed slightly to Alain. "You are a great sorcerer," said he. "If I say I'm sorry, and that I will mend my manners, will you teach me?"

"I might." Alain frowned a little, but he did not seem angry. He said slowly, "I have learned a bit myself tonight. That is dangerous to lose one's temper, when there is power in your hands. I must guard against it in future."

★ ★ ★ ★ ★ ★ ★

In the great hall the sorcerer sat by his fire and read aloud from his book of magic. The hound Dalgard blinked sleepily at his feet. Martin curled against its silky side, playing with the dangling ears. He watched Alain, and thought how wise and kind and splendid he looked; and he watched the prince, sitting on the other side of the hearth, listening attentively, and jotting down notes.

Alain made a slow circle with one hand, and spoke a line from the book. Into the candlelight, firelight, and the moonlight that streamed through the windows, came a brighter glow, which spread and thickened until a Unicorn was standing there. Its horn gleamed. It stretched out a tiny cloven hoof. It whickered.

"Beautiful," said the prince in a whisper. "May I touch it?"

The sorcerer nodded. Avenel put out his hand, and the fabulous creature stooped its lovely head and nuzzled against it with a soft and trembling nose.

Martin was jealous. He had not been allowed to touch the Phoenix. He forgot why. He muttered his little egg-spell.

The unicorn shuddered all over. It said with great hauteur, "Three weeks ago, come Toosday."

It turned blue and vanished.

The sorcerer lifted one slanting eyebrow at his apprentice. Martin gave him an apologetic grin, and slowly turned into a little red cushion.

The hound dropped his head on it, sighed, and went to sleep.

Alain smiled faintly at the prince, and went on reading.